TRIPTYCH

Three Tales of Frontier Horror

By Richard Beauchamp

Edited By Korey Dawson

Cover Art: Don Noble-Rooster Republic Press

For Mark-

The darkness comes for us all in the end, my friend.

Rest In Peace

THE COURIER

The courier waited in the most secluded corner booth of the tavern, eyes fixed outside, watching the snow fall and hearing it tinkle softly off the windows. He had not been sitting long when the door opened, breaking the stillness of the room, and a man with one eye walked in. A natural looming aura entered with him, and the cut of the clothes on his towering frame suggested someone of high esteem. The one-eyed man ordered himself a drink, turning to cast a gaze over the small establishment. When the single roving eye fell upon him, the courier replied with only a terse nod.

They were practically alone in the tavern, but despite this, the client spoke softly, even intimately, as he settled into the seat across the booth.

"You're him, then? Trusted to deliver on time, *every* time?" he asked, taking a long pull of his drink. No introductions, just the smell of ale, but that was fine. The courier already knew his name: Mr. Tiber Ritter. That's what he signed his correspondence with, anyway. The name was vaguely familiar to him, the pages of his mind associating the name with things one would call...*esoteric*. But the mind was a funny thing sometimes.

"Correct," the courier said. "I understand you need this parcel delivered...before the winter solstice?" He matched Ritter's volume and tone, as a courtesy.

"Not a parcel, but a package," Ritter said, producing a satin sack that bulged with some kind of angular object, roughly the size of a pint mug. "A very, *very* valuable one."

He lowered it tenderly onto the table, the object settling

with a heavy weight. The courier noticed the man did not let go of the satin bag. In fact, the gnarled hand had a white knuckle grip on the fabric, his only green eye staring unblinking at the courier.

"It *must* be delivered to my associate on the eve of the solstice," Ritter said. There was a sense of urgency to the man, a tension that filled his movements and his voice. "Absolutely no later. You can guarantee this?"

"Yes," the courier said, meeting the chilling gaze. The man hadn't bothered to cover his empty, scarred socket with a patch, so the courier stared into the shriveled, leaf-like lids as if they had opened around an invisible eye. Again, as a courtesy.

"Now then," Ritter said, finishing his drink in another of those large gulps, wrinkled socket staring. "Name your fee."

"400 dollars for successful, prompt delivery, but a blizzard awaits us. Every day of delinquency I incur would see a deduction, but-"

"I asked, and *you* answered," the one-eyed man said, slamming an open palm on the tabletop. "It will be guaranteed, *boy*, because the late fee for this particular package is your life."

If Ritter had reached to pluck fear from the cheek of the dark face before him, he had come back with an empty fist.

"The matter...*presses*. If my associate does not have this package in his hands by solstice eve, there will be consequences for *everyone*. So I ask again, can you—"

"Yes," the courier repeated, putting out a large, somehow delicate hand, the palm facing up in expectation of currency. "The frontier territories know me as a courier of iron reliability. A man such as you would have sought out an agent of sullied reputation only as readily as having been one himself." The courier felt a momentary delight at the one-eyed man's silence. "Am I wrong?"

"To business, then," Ritter said with a thin smile, producing the agreed upon sum, sliding the package over with a strange, longing look. "Do handle that with *utmost* care."

"I intend to," the courier said, handling the satin carrier with the same delicacy Ritter displayed. "Nothing will be removed or inspected, it will stay just as it is now. Should I ask further questions?" The object was indeed quite heavy, disproportionately so, given its size.

Ritter smiled. "It would make your life incalculably easier if you didn't," he said. "I strongly advise you to not gaze upon the contents." He said, and cast a suspicious look around the empty tavern despite its obvious desolation. "It is also my understanding that your discretion is bought with the same coin as your consistent reliability," Ritter said. "This is to be a private delivery. Are we clear?" The one-eyed man grabbed his hand firmly, rising from the bench.

"Yes," the courier said, shaking on it.

* * *

On his third day of riding, he noticed the interloper.

The courier had chosen a route traversing the Wyoming territories, through several canyons and snow caked gorges. Though the route was a frequently travelled corridor, he hadn't spied a soul along the main route, but on the high walls of those gorges, he finally saw the first. A solitary figure stalked him from there, proceeding with great caution, slipping in and out of the tree line. Whoever it was had stayed just out of sight through central Montana, following the courier south towards the Colorado territories. Jeremiah didn't banter his name about, whether engaged on business or not. It was just "the courier", no more...no less. His face, on the other hand, was something that didn't slip the mind easily anywhere he went, and it wouldn't do to be seen working by anyone except those at the beginning of the money, and those at the end.

His destination was a small mountain town called

Breckenridge, with instructions to deliver the package to a man named Tobias Wicker, who he was told would be awaiting him at his estate. He had never been this far south before, as most of his deliveries brought him up around the Canadian territories, but the courier stayed apprised of the political climate concerning folks of his kind. The many sprawling trade routes that crawled across the continent held different risks, and it was to his understanding that this was a safe route.

So, he pretended to feign obliviousness to the interloper's presence, and Maude didn't give a damn either way. Jeremiah focused instead on navigating the harsh terrain ahead of him, paying attention to her body language, and reading the creature so he didn't end up with a lamed beast and a potential delay. He'd hoped coming south would mean more temperate climates, but the frigidity of the far north had followed him down. Despite the growing blizzard he'd been fighting through, his stalker did not abate, and matched his relentless pace, if not his chattering teeth.

It was on the fourth day when the man approached, hands open in a sign of peace. He materialized out of the swirling white wall that encompassed the courier's vision on all sides, walking at a comfortable gait towards the makeshift camp. The man was not a native, but European, his thick cattle hide duster billowing about him as he pulled down his scarf to speak.

The courier did not move, staring at the man from across the smoldering fire he'd recently cooked a humble breakfast over. Frozen in the act of packing Maude's saddle bags, he slowly put his hands into the pockets of his own coat, carefully flexing the frozen tendons in his fingers.

"Howdy, friend," the man bellowed, walking up to kneel by the fire. He lowered his hands over the glowing red coals, hiding from the ever-howling, ever biting wind.

"State your business," the courier replied, hands clenching and unclenching in those warm pockets.

"It is to my understanding that you have in your possession

a package. One delivered unto you by a man named Tiber Ritter. Am I correct in that regard?" The man yelled over the sound of the wind, each word sending out a dense plume of steam that was quickly ripped away by the stream of mountain air.

"Until you tell me who you are, I am not obligated to confirm any such thing to you," the courier said, opening the flexing fingers in his right pocket just long enough to grip something heavy instead.

"I'm an interested third party. Tell me, boy, do you have any idea what you have in your possession?" the man asked. Standing up from the fire, he set his hands to wrangling the flapping edges of his coat in, then thrust them into deep pockets of his own to disappear. The courier didn't respond, but looked around instead, trying to see if the man was alone. Everything beyond twenty feet just looked like so much swirling ivory. "It is an abominable thing, really. The same can be said for the man you're delivering it to, but only one needs to be destroyed...for now. Tell me, what'd he pay for your services? I can double—"

"I am not parting ways with it. My contracts are non-negotiable, and the package is not for sale," the courier said.

"That's unfortunate," the man said, setting his jaw. "I'm afraid I won't be leaving you until it is in my possession. You don't understand what you've got there, boy. It goes beyond the bounds of your contract, regardless of the money, or the worthless reputation of a name. Follow through, and there's gonna be—"

The last word was like a dinner bell for chaos. Maude gave a blustery cry of distress, followed by the sound of a third pair of stumbling feet in the snow. Wincing at this, the interloper knew the game was up, and what was sure to come after. Time dilated to a crawl, and the courier registered the look of impending violence in his opponent's face, but he wasted no quarter.

A red firework blazed in the interloper's chest, an explosion of color in the endless white. The wind helped in these matters, and the courier's draw was well practiced. He'd seen the man's own revolver catch on his billowing coat as he tried to pull free. Just as the man fell limp in the snow, he saw the other man in silhouette.

"Stop!" the courier barked. The accomplice had snuck up on Maude from behind on a last ditch attempt and had managed to grab the damned package. He could see it pendulum in the wind, the pointed satin fabric catching snowflakes, quickly melting into little puffs of steam as they touched it. The horse bucking from the shot allowed the accomplice take advantage of the chaos, then make a run for it. He was ten steps away, but the command and the flash of gun metal had stopped him in his tracks.

The courier hadn't been inclined to hear the man out, but would take pause for the wind to at least settle a bit. Watching the swaying of the satin, the courier timed the opening so he wouldn't hit the package as well. The figure took one step forward, his open mouth a black smudge.

"This is not your element. You couldn't possibly understand the consequences of what you're doing, you—" The gun spoke once more, cutting off the words. The accomplice spun violently in the air, the package turning with him as he crashed down, face first in the snow.

Jeremiah took a brief moment to settle his agitated horse, and then went to the man he'd shot last, rolling the body over and looking for the package. Carefully prying it from the dying man's grasp, he was dismayed to see that a good amount of blood had soaked into the dark fabric. He held it up to his face, watching the dark, wet splotches disappear before his very eyes, the cloth becoming very warm indeed. Jeremiah stared at it for a second, then searched the bodies, looking for something to identify them or their intent, but he found nothing besides ammunition and provisions, and no evidence of any nearby horses.

He approached Maude carefully, and she snorted twin gouts of steam, whinnying as he got closer. She was still skittish from the brief battle, he thought, placing the package carefully back in its satchel.

"Easy, girl," Jeremiah said. She continued to shy away from him when he tried to secure the package in the saddle bag. Package finally secure, he began to hastily pack up camp.

The next twenty miles or so were rough going, fierce winds biting through every layer he'd wrapped himself in, pushing him and Maude around as they descended through a mountain pass, their pace slow and cautious. He had done the calculations for the journey as soon as he'd received the letter, making sure it was even possible. That had been a week ago, and though he'd factored inclement weather into his travels, he had not accounted for a full-blown blizzard. It would be a matter of either upping his pace to cut through the ever-growing snow drifts and risking his horse fouling a leg, or going slow and steady, with the risk of falling behind schedule.

As he once again recalled the conversation they'd had in the inn, Tiber's words came back to him, but the face was different. It wasn't a mouth speaking in front of him, but a voice issuing from a flat drawing, like a dream.

The realization came to Jeremiah like a flash, instantly remembering where he'd heard the name, and had seen that haunted visage before he had ever sat down across from it. A wanted poster hung outside a courthouse in Billings. A rough sketch of a ghastly man with one eye. *WANTED- TIBER CORNELIOUS RITTER- KIDNAPPING, INCITING VIOLENCE, KNOWN PRACTITIONER OF OCCULT ARTS. BOUNTY: $600.*

He'd seen that poster what, some six months ago? And what did that change? The courier had delivered mail and packages for known outlaws and miscreants before, and would have been a broke man indeed if he hadn't.

Maude cried out suddenly, nearly bucking him from his saddle, but he held on to the beast's neck, grabbing tight and yelling for her to hold. They'd slipped into a large drift just as they'd come to the bottom of the mountain, and the poor girl sunk up to her shoulders in snow, snorting in a panic.

"Go on, girl, it's okay...it's alright," he said. Jeremiah tried to spur her sides with his boots, but his legs from calf to feet were nothing but frozen, numb meat, and he could barely manage to twitch them. But she continued on, practically swimming through the snow drifts, the courier fastidiously checking the saddle bag every few miles to make sure his mail was still secured. By the time they broke through, they were back on level ground, and he could see a half-buried signpost reading GLENROCK-3 MILES DUE SOUTH.

Relief washed over him at the sight. Traversing unfamiliar land in a world that was so much rolling white, the cold had made it hard to think straight. He'd been half convinced he'd gotten himself lost, and had known another hour or two out here would have meant frostbite on one or both of them. Jeremiah spurred the horse on once more, eager to get out of the cold.

As he began to see the vague shapes of buildings materializing out of the gloom, he thought of the blood that had seeped into the bag. At that, he brought Maude to a stop, and turned to dig into his right saddle bag, grabbing the soft fabric and the impossibly heavy instrument within for the umpteenth time that day. It was now almost hot to the touch. For a moment, he held it against him, treasuring the warmth, his eyes examining the fabric once more for signs of stain or aberration. There was none.

Jeremiah felt something then, as he held the package, its mysterious properties suddenly becoming quite fascinating to him. The urge to rip open the puckered rim of the drawstring and gaze inside was almost maddening. He blinked rapidly and shook his head, remembering why he'd taken it out in the first place. The courier took the draw strings and tied them in a sturdy knot around the belt of his pants. His encounter with the interlopers on the mountain told him this business concerned more than just the agreed upon parties. He would have to be careful going into town, and had to assume more men privy to his delivery would be trying to ambush him.

It sat heavy and hot against his leg as he trundled into town, people milling about around him, kicking through the accumulated snow drifts. A barker on one corner of a tall building exclaimed in great puffs of steam how the Rousted Bull was selling their special ale by the pint for a steeply discounted price for today only. Children played in the snow off to his left, tossing snowballs at one another, giggling when a hit was scored. Two men sat on elevated porches, surveying their small jurisdiction of town square with solemn expressions, smoking pipes and huddling against the cold. They nodded to the courier as he passed, and he nodded back, assuming everyone was an enemy.

He found an inn at the edge of Glenrock that appeared sparsely occupied, and tied Maude off at the accompanying saddle post. The courier went inside, sighing with relief at the cozy warmth of the place, the large fire roaring in the hearth and illuminating two men playing chess nearby. A woman rose behind the counter, plump with child, her eyes going wide at the snow-caked wraith before her.

"My goodness, sir, you look half frozen to death!" she said. "Are you alright?" He approached the counter, dropping bits of melting snow on the floorboards, and pulled back a frozen flap of jacket for his coin purse. The woman's eyes darted to the bulging sack tied to his pants. She flinched suddenly, holding her belly and wincing slightly as he pulled out money. "Blazes, he's a-kicking," she said, under her breath.

"I'll rally," the courier said. "How much for one

night?"

The woman cleared her throat and regained her composure, one hand still cradling the distended belly. "That'll be...uh...four dollars," she said, her voice suddenly tight.

"You alright, ma'am?" he asked, not liking the way her eyes kept shifting to the satin bag.

"Yeah, sorry...he's kickin' up a storm today, my goodness." She spoke with a shaky laugh, but had no trouble taking his money, and reached under the counter for a brass key. "Room 23, up the stairs and to your right. Biscuits, gravy and hot coffee will be served at sunrise." Nodding a pleasant dismissal, the woman sat down heavily on a nearby wooden chair, and grimaced again. The courier walked past the wizened old men at the chessboard, their rheumy eyes following him. Making his way slowly up to the room, he felt the stares drawing a bead on him, but knew they were the usual fare associated with those of his kind. Men usually under the yoke of their owners.

He found his room and quickly shrugged off his clothes. The pain made him wince as he untied the package from his waist, delicately placing it onto a small table beside the bed, and stiffly peeled off his trousers. A blistered, irritated patch of skin had erupted where the package had rested against his hip. He went about lancing the small white boils with his knife, carefully rinsing the area using the humble wash basin that sat unused in one corner of the room, gritting his teeth at the process. A peculiar physiological manifestation, he thought. His mind turned over why and how his skin had been burned like that, but in the end, he was too tired to ruminate on such matters, and felt his head nodding almost immediately.

As he sunk into his pillow, he hoped beyond hope that he would be free of nightmares. He was not a man prone to night terrors, his sleep normally abyssal and dreamless. Since the beginning of the journey in the company of the package, however, he found himself plagued by vivid flashbulb dreams of his old life, the one he did his best to forget about. A man speaking quick, calling off numbers, origins of birth, and pedigrees, as if they had been prized racehorses and not humans. The crack of a whip. The cry of his mother as she was whisked away from him, the announcer congratulating the man who won her. *A fine breeder, that one there.*

* * *

The courier came down the stairs just as the sun was beginning to paint the sky a bruised purple over the horizon, and as promised, the delicious smells of a home-cooked breakfast greeted him as he entered the lobby. He had moved the package to the pocket of his coat, sacrificing the extra bit of security of fastening it to his person, if only to spare himself another hellish lancing. Carefully surveying the room, he saw a small family of four filling up a table in one corner, the ancient chess players in evidence nearby. If not for the gravy that spattered their beards, they could have been statues of themselves from the night before. A small serving table had been setup in one corner, and the courier fixed himself a plate and a cup of steaming hot coffee.

He ate in silence, the eyes around him drilling an itchy little spot into the back of his neck. Glancing at the pregnant woman in the back corner, the courier noted a young man flanking her that he presumed to be the husband and owner. Their eyes shifted away when he looked their way, and he began to eat hastily, wanting to be on the road and gone. Tension filled the room like the smoke of a burning hotcake. He could feel the woman walking over as he finished his plate, almost knocking into her as he stood up, yanking his coat from the back of the chair.

"May I take your plate for you?" she asked.

Something fell at their feet with a *thunk* and both of them looked down to see the satin drawstring bag on the floor. She stooped to pick it up with a quickness that stunned him.

"Oh my, let me just—"

"*Stop!*" the courier said, reaching for her, but it was too late.

The woman cried out as her hand touched the bag, stumbling back as if she'd been jack-slapped. She bumped into the table behind her, crying out and holding her belly. A dark red flower blossomed on the front of her dress as she fell on her behind, a thick, coppery smell creeping up over the savory smells of food in the room.

"Loretta!" the young man cried, running over to her. Loretta collapsed to the ground, blood beginning to pool out from between her legs.

"It's the baby, James, *Oh..*," she gasped, "Something... something's happening to the baby..," She groaned, scrunching her face up in excruciating pain, red fingers clasped at her belly. The courier was quickly stowing away the package as he tried to get out of there, all eyes on him now. But the man whirled on him, grabbing the lapels of his jacket.

"*You!* Who even let you in here, you *Got*-damned mongrel?" He lunged into the courier's face, almost snarling. "What'd you do to my wife, you fuckin' n—"

He briskly shoved her husband back, hand clenching over his pocket as he ran for the door, determined not to lose it again. Loretta cried out once more, a hoarse, ragged sound of primal agony echoing in his ears. The courier backed over the threshold, then turned and ran for his horse.

The icy morning air reached the depth of his lungs, biting into his chest as he sprinted to a stop beside a startled Maude, pulling taut at the post. Sliding home into his stirrups, gasping until pain knifed into his ribs, the courier whipped around to see a gaggle of men filing out of the inn at speed. He counted the flintlock pistols being primed, some armaments he didn't recognize, and even a blunderbuss being aimed in his direction as he kicked off. The animal read the panic in him and started a brisk gallop towards the south end of town.

He understood then, as he rode off towards the climbing peaks to the south, that shelter in any sort of civilized environment was impossible. At least, not while in possession of the abominable thing which was his charge. Once again surrounded by snow encrusted conifers and jagged snow-capped peaks, a sense of dread excitement filled him. Jeremiah realized that he was in possession of something truly awesome in its power, something that defied his rough understanding of the world and the boundaries of what was considered to be "real".

He rode for as long as Maude would let him, putting some forty miles between him and Glenrock that day, only stopping at one of the three outposts he passed through to resupply her with feed for the journey ahead. He rode into the night, the blizzard giving way to a cold snap that froze the once-powdery snow drifts into hard, treacherous crusts of ice. Poor Maude scraped her legs into ribbons as they rode down the southern express trade route, only seeing one or two wagons fool enough to make this perilous journey themselves.

That night, Jeremiah found a small stone outcropping to sleep under passing through the gorge of yet another valley, the tedious task of starting and maintaining a fire leaving him dog tired by the time he settled in for the night. His hands were sticky and numb from pine resin and his nose ran until a thick crust of ice coated his upper lip. He got the fire as big as he could make it, but even still, he was frozen to the marrow as he huddled deep into the buckskin sleeping bag.

At some point in the night, the fire had gone out. Jeremiah laid shivering, too cold and tired to get it going again. He curled into a tight ball deep inside his sleeping bag, the air and the ground leeching every last ounce of warmth from his body. The thought of the package crept into his mind unbidden, how warm it would be, cradled against his chest. *No, you can't.*

You risk madness. You risk giving in to temptation, he thought. Even as he warned himself against it, he found himself crawling from his sleeping bag, the cold against his flesh a profound and breathtaking force. He stumbled shivering over to Maude, who also visibly trembled in the cold.

"Sorry girl, I n...n...need this," he chattered, pulling the package from the saddle bag, and Christ, that warmth. Jeremiah cradled it against his body like a newborn child, almost weeping with the blessed heat that radiated from it. He crawled back into his sleeping bag, not caring if he awoke with all the sores in the world, and closed his eyes. His mind plunged back into the auctioneer's raffle, back into that childhood memory he thought he'd suppressed long ago.

* * *

The courier awoke to the sounds of mastication, of flesh rending and tearing. He came awake with a start, hands groping for his gun and prying open his frozen eyelids. His surroundings were washed in a pale gray monochrome as the moon rose small but bright in the Yukon sky. The meaty ripping noise abruptly stopped, and in its place a low, guttural hiss emerged. He knew what it was even before he got his sight about him.

Crouching defensively, the mountain lion inched towards the courier through a great cloud of steam, twitching its gore-flecked lips. The sinewy body padded around a gaping red crater torn from the body of the prostrate horse, dark crimson splashed across the frozen snow from Maude's own geyser. How the courier hadn't woken from the commotion sooner was beyond him. He tried to grasp the flint lock with frozen digits, numb and stupid in their scrabbling, clawing for a handhold on the wooden stock.

The cat slunk forward, ears back, whiskers glistening with blood in the pale light. It could've lunged for him, but hesitated as if skirting a transparent wall. Either it was already sated from the horse's innards, or something undetected by the senses of man was keeping it at bay. It bore its teeth, primal weaponry caked with flesh and intestine, strands of horse hair caught in its gums.

The package, he thought. He had cradled it protectively all night, despite what it had done to the landlady and the life inside of her, and now it was gone. The courier clawed around in the snow like a man in a dark room, not taking his eyes from the slinking death before him, then tore the bag from the white crust. Grasping the thing inside for dear life, he thrust it out in front of him, impossibly warm in his useless hand. The mist around the bag began to thicken with a faint luminescent sheen, lighting the cat's eyes like two small portals to hell.

The big cat immediately backpedaled, swatting ham-sized paws at the air, its claws like hayhooks. There was five feet between him and the animal, but it moved to knock the bag away furiously, as if it were errant coals from the fire. It let out one hissing plume, high and indignant like a house cat, then turned away. The courier watched it bound silently into the ivory hellscape, leaving him flustered, half-frostbitten, and down a horse...the only thing he called a friend.

As his heartbeat slowed, Jeremiah understood that nothing could come to hurt him while in the presence of the object, and the nagging temptation to look inside the bag came flooding back to him. This was no longer just a package, and he no longer just its temporary charge, a middleman between two clients. This thing had protected him, as well as put him in mortal danger.

A talisman....My...Talisman, he thought deliriously, finding his trembling fingers reaching to loosen the drawstrings, to peer at the marvelous object inside...

He shook his head violently and his whole body quaked, summoning an iron tang of willpower to make himself drop the bag. There was an almost magnetic pull to it, and he knew offloading it was vital, for he would not be able to resist its calling much longer. He forced himself to shove the object back in his pocket, aware of a throbbing, burning wetness on his chest and arms, but dared not peel off his garments to inspect what he knew would be festering there.

In a daze, Jeremiah got to his feet, going over to the eviscerated horse and quickly scavenging all he could carry into his pockets. He'd been on the road for what, ten days now? And he was only just now crossing over into the Colorado divide. He didn't know how far away from Breckenridge he was now, but to his understanding, the township was in the heart of the state. It was a sovereign town ran by one man, isolated from the established outposts.

He had four days to get where he was going, and on foot at that. Jeremiah ran blindly into the dark, following the barely discernable trail trampled down by so many wagons and horses over the years. Despite the frigid cold, he went on, growing numb to everything. A light euphoria usurped the physiological discomforts he'd been suffering as he bordered on hypothermia, ice reaching down into the marrow of his bones. He remembered some years ago, he'd been shot in the right arm, a wound from a disagreement between owner and recipient of a parcel. A morphine tincture had been administered to ease the pain, the back alley doctor pulling the round from his flesh with whisky-soaked tweezers.

It was that light footed, warm and fuzzy bliss he felt now, and understood that it was the object's doing. Protecting him, allowing him to go on, to surpass the physical limits of his body.

"My talisman..." he groaned aloud as he plunged onward, disappearing into the white abyss.

* * *

In the small mountain town of Mayberry, people cringed and stepped away. As he shuffled over the rough-hewn street, many mistook him for a leper on account of the open, weeping pustules coating his hands and face.

"Need to find... Breckenridge..," he moaned aloud, asking various people who dared get close enough where the town was. The only one who was brave enough to stop him was the town priest, who saw the man as sick in the mind and heart, sure the healing touch of God would set the travelling vagrant right.

"Breckenridge..." the courier repeated. "Do you know where..."

"Whoa, whoa...easy there, sir. What's the hurry? What is in Breckenridge that is so important?" the priest asked patiently. The courier looked at him, irises eclipsed by the dark holes of his dilated pupils. His one exposed hand trembled, the nails and tips of his fingers black from frost bite, while the other was hidden deep in his tattered coat, clenching something fiercely.

"Must go...d-deliver package...buh...Breckenridge..," he stuttered.

"Son... Breckenridge is a haven for sinners. The black heart of Satan lives there. Are you in league with the devil, son?" he asked. The Courier looked up at him, his gaunt face staring uncomprehending into the priest's eyes.

"Just t-tell me...*p-please*. Important business. Very... important," he said. The priest gave him a thin smile and pointed a long, bony hand straight ahead, towards the edge of town.

"Six miles due southeast of here. If you step foot into Breckenridge, do not ever come back here. This is a God-fearing community of fine Christian folk, and what goes on over in that God-forsaken town would...you'd...be bringing corruption back here if you visit that place, and that heathen of a man who resides there, the devil incarnate, and I won't be having any of that," he said, but the words were spoken to the courier's back. He was already shambling in that direction, a miasma of rot and unwashed man-flesh trailing after him.

* * *

Jeremiah had been travelling in something of a daze since the encounter with the mountain lion, his feet trudging onwards towards some unknowable direction. The shape inside the bag guided him, unseeing, pulling towards their destination with some unseen tidal force. It was no longer just a package, no longer just an object, but his talisman. A voice without a mouth called out to him, just as something called to the talisman itself. As they grew closer, the pull became more persistent, and he realized he would soon have to surrender the thing, now beloved, to a third party.

The original purpose of his journey was long forgotten, his body instead following the ebbing tides that flowed through his talisman. His soul was now a fish caught in an oceanic current, mindlessly following the path of all things, across all time. It wasn't until he'd stumbled into the small village, which bore no sign post or population sign, that he realized he'd finally reached his destination. The courier was taken into the arms of a crowd of red-robed figures at the threshold, welcoming him with reverent whispers. He was swept off his feet, which had long ago shed their boots and were missing several digits, and was carried towards the largest structure of the whole village. Looking blearily towards the sky as he floated towards his destiny, the courier saw the ghostly orb of the moon, daring to show its face while the sun was still out.

An ancient voice boomed all around him. "By the gods, he has come. Our messenger!" it said, and the scenery changed from blue endless sky to tall canvas ceilings, upon which the shadows of flames danced.

They set him down gently against the ground, and he could feel several boils rupture and wet his back. It was nothing to him. The talisman protected him from pain, from...everything.

His eyes rolled in his head as a solitary figure loomed over him, a face etched with the valleys and canyons of time, eyes milky with cataracts. It gazed down at him, through him, and pale, ashen lips split the craggy face open into a toothless grin. A ghastly sight to behold, the ghoulish facsimile of a man reached out to him with trembling, liver-spotted hands.

The courier batted weakly at the robed congregants who searched his person, but he did not have the strength to stop them. One of them found the satin bag and tore it free, the heart of it now glowing brightly red, and handed it to the wizened man. *Tobias Wicker himself*, he thought.

"No..," he groaned, reaching out for it, his talisman.

A look of total reverence came over Tobias's face as he beheld the object, pulling open the draw strings. "It's...*mine...*" the ancient man said, pausing to give the courier a look of pity, of understanding. "Ah yes... I see you've bonded with it. Anyone who has shown devotion to it will be endowed with its protection. It is easy to be confused in this. You see, it is sentient, and it understands when it is being guarded, and will do likewise. But you...my poor boy. You are but the messenger, its deliverer. A pivotal role in this whole event...but, alas, you are not worthy of its true power. Only those of us who've glimpsed beyond the veil, and palavered with its creators, shall share a true connection with it. To withstand its awesome aura, which, to the uninitiated like you, can have ghastly effects on your physiognomy," he said, reaching into the bag.

The courier's eyes opened wide as he watched Tobias pull it out, at long last letting him glimpse what he'd been dying to witness. At first, he was blinded by the brilliant crimson aura, which shone like a miniature sun in the small yurt, and several gasps and exhaled breaths sounded, noises of pure awe and elation.

"I see you've been fed recently. Supped from the blood of both man and beast. Very good. That is a good start, but...I sense the growing hunger within you. There, there," Tobias said to it, as if consoling a small child. The glow became less dazzling, sinking into a darker, deeper hue, the color of arterial blood, and the courier could see it more clearly.

A square-sided rune, made out of what appeared to be obsidian, or some other dark, glistening rock. Several complex shapes that glowed with the red aura were etched into the rock, beautiful geometric formations that swirled and reformed with a hypnotic rhythm.

"What...what *is* it?" the courier whispered.

"A *key*," Tobias said. "A key to other worlds, to other dimensions. To doors of infinite perception." He released the cube high above him, to float in the center of the yurt. "And tonight... on this eve of hibernal solstice, when we are at our farthest from our home star, we shall open one door in particular. They shall come on the tide of the midnight sun, and flood this land with purity. What others call abominations, demons even...we call *gods*, and they will rape our new religion into the masses," he said, his voice growing tremulous with reverence.

The courier barely registered this rambling dialogue as all the pain and physical injury so mercifully stricken from him before came flooding back. A red blaze pierced the void around the rune, consolidating into a rectangular set of glowing vertices. The further away it moved from him, the more he was allowed to feel his own nerve endings and pain receptors again, its numbing aura bending into hellish geometry before him. The pain was breathtaking, his extremities burning with their gangrenous rot. He felt every single blister and throbbing pustule merge into one pulsing lightning bolt of pain. Every beat of his heart meant agony, and he groaned, for it was all he could do.

"The door is almost open, but it must feed fully to truly bend the dimensions together. Are you all, my loyal flock, ready to make the ultimate sacrifice?" Tobias asked.

"Yes, master," the chorus of human voices said, with no

hesitation. They circled around him, disrobing themselves. Naked forms of various shapes and sizes, both male and female, stood about him, ornate ceremonial blades in their hands. Tobias knelt down next to his deliverer, putting a hand on his forehead, the other suddenly filled with a blade of its own.

"Jeremiah Amalhe, that is your name, yes?" Tobias said, every grimy tooth set free. It had been so long since he'd heard his own name aloud that at first, all he could do was blink. "Ye...yes," Jeremiah stammered.

"Do you willingly give up your corporeal vessel to serve it? This, which is to be our own Pandora's Box?"

"*Yes,*" Jeremiah said, immediately. Anything to connect himself with it once more, anything to make the pain stop, every nerve ending in his body screaming. He stared up at the shimmering red void, thinking it a most beautiful sight.

The blade moved soundlessly, parting the flesh of his throat, his trachea sundered under its gleaming edge. A white-hot line of agony barely registered among the litany of others endured in that moment. As blood filled his lungs, he watched the others do likewise, great red geysers erupting in unison, the infinite droplets only to float like crimson snow in the air.

Mesmerized in his death throes, Jeremiah gazed wordlessly as all the blood came together and flowed upwards instead. Gravity held no power in the small canvas yurt, with dark rivers gushing from the eager throats towards the scarlet doorway above. Ravenous for the life force, the portal grew more vivid, more substantial...more real. Just as his vision faded to red, Jeremiah saw something gaze back at him from behind the void. An indescribable, monstrous face at the membrane between worlds, pushing its way out of its dimension, and into that of his.

BLOOD GULCH

"Where is he, grub?" Maylene panted, the big barrel of her revolver heavy in her hand. She rested it against the mottled scar on the nape of the man's neck, reminding Bennet that violence was in there with them. The claustrophobic stone walls of his hideout squeezed closer with the fetid anticipation of it, like the coil of a snake.

"Told you…the gulch. He's at the gu—"

She pulled back the revolver's hammer. In the small room, the sound may as well have been a thunderclap. Facing true death, the man squirmed against his restraints.

"Lot of gulches between here and San Marsito. Be specific, slug."

His lips were the color of spoiled pork chops, twitching into a bad smile.

"Blood Gulch. You know where. It's where they take everyone," he sneered, boiled eggs where his eyes should have been, the yolks sliding her direction.

Maylene swallowed, looking over at Raul. He nodded, staring over darkened eyelids as she turned back to the chair-bound man, his once moussed pompadour plastered to an ash white forehead.

"Tell me," Maylene said, her voice betraying just a hint of a waver, "My husband. Did y'all… is he…like *you* now? Answer true, and I'll make it quick."

"No, we no touch him. He special. He saved… for other things," said the man once known as Bennet Tilson, formerly of the Brush Creek Sons Gang. "Please...let me go, I take you to him. I —"

"No need, slug, I know where Blood Gulch is," Raul said, stepping forward. "Put 'im below snakes, Maylene. I'll hold his head."

"What?" Bennet gasped, eyes making like tea saucers, body thrashing. Maylene's thin lips, ones that never saw a dab of lipstick in her life, turned up in a vicious grin as she put her iron away. In its stead she took out the silver bowie knife. Teeth popped in the bound man's jaw at the sight of it. "No. NO, N—" The blade glinted in the candlelight as Raul grabbed the big man's head, yanking it down so his nape was exposed.

"I'm gonna make it bad for you. For wasting my time. And... just cause I feel like it," Maylene hissed into his ear. The façade was fully dropped now, and Bennet started making markedly inhuman noises as she moved the blade's wicked tip down, carefully cutting around the scar in the man's neck. She was practiced at this particular butchery, ensuring surgical precision.

Peeling back layers of skin and muscle, she saw the wriggling red bulge lodged in the brain stem, that most unwelcome passenger. Maylene carefully levered the knife around the nasty little sucker of its mouth like a crowbar to a whiskey crate, and with a *plop*, dislodged it from its comfy little nest of nerve endings and muscle tissue. A high pitched squeal like a soprano piglet pierced the silence. Maylene grabbed the four-inch-long grub right below the head, the way you grab a surly rattler, and pulled it free.

They were like leeches if leeches were things born from Hell and not the Earth, with a corpulent ruby-red body and a lamprey's mouth lined with rows of fine needle teeth. Sumbitches could burrow into you one night with you being none the wiser 'til you woke up looking out of eyes that weren't your own.

Maylene pulled out the small packet of salt she kept in her ration bag, she had plenty of jerky to spare for such things, and tore off a corner with her teeth. Predicting its demise, the little bastard thrashed and squirmed, but Maylene held tight. She poured the salt on, the effect instantaneous, like a match to flash powder. The skin began to smoke and bubble up, the thing swelling like a bullfrog's throat mid-croak.

They both looked away as she dropped it, the thing exploding with a wet pop, leaving a gooey mess and an unholy stink.

"Blood Gulch. Heard about it, never been...how long a ride?" Maylene said. The Brush Creek camp was *way* off the beaten trail.

"You ain't never been 'cause it's a place you don't wanna go," Raul said. "Twenty miles south of here, near the border of the Nevada territories, but the last three's on foot. They spot us coming in—" He clamped his mouth shut, rubbing the back of his neck. It was all that needed to be said.

"You with me?" Maylene asked, packing up.

"Always. John was a good man...even if he did want to see me hang by my *cajones.* Not many left like 'im. Plus, those little fuckers got my Louisa. I'll kill as many as I can...then ventilate myself just to keep them from having a warm body."

"I won't let that happen," Maylene said, locking onto his eyes. "Hell is what they left behind, and we'll make sure it's given back to 'em."

* * *

They made their way across the great Sonoran plains, the sun a malicious thing in the sky, intent on cooking them alive in their leathers, with an occasional saguaro promising piss-warm bitter water if they got that desperate. Their donkeys, surly things with the languid disposition of house cats, went on at a snail's pace. Maylene was half tempted to go the rest of the way on foot.

"How come you was able to go in this place, it's so bad," she asked, "And get back without one o' them red riders in you?"

"My outfit was riding through the same county where the cave-in happened." Raul said, trying without success to spur his lazy donkey to speed.

"E-day, you mean?" Maylene said, shedding her duster, willing to risk sunburn over impending heat stroke.

"Si. As I recall, your husband was actually on our trail at the time, meaning to take in our boss, Rodriguez, for that botched stickup in Albuquerque. *Los niños perdidos* was always good at laying low."

"That you were," Maylene said flatly.

"Hey, I wasn't so good at sticking my head in the sand, never would've ended up in that *ghoss* town and save you...*no*?" Raul reminded her, taking a swig from his water skin.

"True," Maylene said, remembering that day well. She'd been on the hunt for John, who'd disappeared for parts unknown trying to find the source of the red rider scourge, and tracked him to an abandoned farm town called Cougher's Bend. It had been a mining camp that had grown, then gone to seed long before the worm-plague, and there, Maylene had found only death. The slugs, markedly better at piloting their human vessels in the few months since E-day, had set an ambush for her. Four of them had her pinned down, prying her mouth open and dangling a slug inches away from her face, when Raul came in, guns blazing. The Lost Boys Gang had been near the top of John "Two Shot" Baker's shit-list, but Maylene, a recent convert to her husband's bounty hunter business, decided his rescue had balanced the books.

"We were there, watching from the saloon, the day those *estupido* miners broke through into their caverns. They all came out, walking like they were drunk, acting strange. Thought nothing of it at the time, didn't say shit when the townspeople went bad. Then one day, I wake up still drunk from a one night stand with a bottle of Soro, find the whole town was migrating, *mi hermanos* in tow. Is funny, really. Almoss get kick out of gang for drinking, and yet, its the one thing that save me. I follow them at a distance, herd of shambling people. Follow them for miles, all the way back to Blood Gulch. Camp out on a ridge for a few days, observing, drinking. The Gulch goes underground, big cave down there. *Big*. Saw them bringing people down, hogtied or in handcuffs. Lots of people. Didn't see them come back out. Then those fucking *jinet rojo* got the hang of being human. Got smart. Post lookouts. I almost got caught. Now? Is guarded like Fort fuckin' Knox."

It was the most she'd ever heard Raul speak, and this news frosted her spine, despite the dry oven they were roasting alive in.

"You think they're using 'em... for food? Gotta eat something," she said, dreading the answer, but Raul just shrugged.

"Dunno. All I know is, people are taken down there, and they don't come out."

They rode on in silence then, Maylene thinking of her life before E-day. She was the first woman sheriff to ever run law over in Possum, where she and John had laid down roots. Took folks awhile to kin to a woman runnin' law, but they knew her husband, and knew if they ever gave her shit, John would hear of it, and big John Two Shot (named for his sawed off double barrel, which never left his side) was not a man you wanted to anger. But just when she had restored some order to the border town, E-day happened. The slugs moved slow, but they bred fast, and learned how to usurp their human cattle quickly. John and a few others had heard of the plague moving through, and always a seeker of justice, he decided to swap his bounty hunter hat for one of pest control. Bullheaded sumbitch, that was her husband.

The first few weeks it was easy to tell who was who. Those that had a rider on 'em shambled and drooled and made about like invalids. But quickly, the little red grubs learned, until it was almost impossible to tell who was whole and which had the red passenger. Now, if you had some man riding up on you with guns pulled, it was a 50/50 toss-up as to whether it was a bonafide *bandido* or a red rider come trying to find another warm body for their brood. Only way to tell these days was by the scars of the neck.

* * *

"Up this way, got a place we can camp. Overlooks the gulch," Raul said, aiming his donkey towards a rising bluff ahead. As they climbed and Maylene got a better look, she realized they were climbing up one wall of the gulch. Down below, she saw the red valley where a river had run long ago, now gone as dry as a whore's giblets at confessional. Raul abruptly held up a fist, *stop*, and dismounted. Maylene did the same, suddenly noticing the strange way he walked, sliding his feet along like a shambling drunk.

"What—"

"They got ways of tellin' someone coming. Cave site is still a few miles away, but this close, they got sentries. Don't know how they do it," Raul said, leaning down to scoop sand into his palm. "Maybe grubs in the ground listening, like a hive, some shit. But they know footsteps," he said, and slapped his forearm, vibrating the mound through his fingers.

"Gotta walk all drunk-like...draggin' your feet. Confuse them. Makes you an animal to them. Don't know why, juss know it work. Grab your bedroll and whatever you need for a day's camp," he whispered.

So Maylene loaded up. Water skin. Few hunks of jerky and hard tack. Two pocketfuls of high yield slug hunter rounds for her irons. Bedroll. The last of the whiskey. And the bandana. Couldn't forget that.

* * *

By the time they made it to the lookout, Maylene's legs quivered like a newborn calf's. After the mile or so of "drunk-walking", they ached something fierce, Charlie-horse cramps seizing her all the way up to her buttocks like a drunken horndog with a marrow-deep touch. When they finally reached the lip of the valley wall, she collapsed in a heap, not caring if all the slugs in the world knew she was there.

The sun was just starting to crawl behind the mountains to the west, buttering the ragged horizon with a vivid orange light. She was grateful to see it go.

"*Psst,*" Raul hissed, motioning her towards the lip. He gave Maylene the spyglass, probably pilfered off some dead boat captain with a slit throat, and pointed with a calloused finger. What she saw through the eye-piece made her jaw drop.

It was like a slaver's train, except 'stead of natives and escaped black folks in chains led by a surly white fella, it was a hodge-podge of people of all cut and carriage. The children were the worst...at least three of them, chained together with a gaggle of adults of all types. The slugs didn't care who or what you were. If you walked on two feet and talked, you were fair game.

"We gotta set 'em free!" she said, ignoring her rubber legs as she tried to get up, but Raul roughly pulled her back down.

"No-no, *chica...* You do that, we're fucked. Watch," he said, and Maylene did.

The procession crossed under a rock arch, where four men stood guard with Sharps carbines, the repeating kind. Behind them, the adobe earth opened up like a bloody mouth, waiting to swallow those poor souls whole.

"So, what do we do?" Maylene asked, feeling hopeless, like she was fighting an unwinnable war. The slug infestation was spreading fast. From Missouri down to Louisiana, huge blockades and wooden walls kept anyone from the west out. Last she heard, Sheriff Horton over in Kansas City, one of John's many correspondents, reported red rider encounters via his last telegram, even with the enforced quarantine. It was like trying to keep the sand out of a desert shithouse.

"Early morning, right before sun come up. Coldest part of the day. Something about the cold...slows 'em down. Guards go in to feed, whatever they do down there. We sleep and wait. Go in when gate empty," Raul said, pint bottle of tequila open before she saw his hand move. He took his evening medicine, and Maylene joined him with her own.

For whatever reason, the slugs hated alcohol. They wouldn't touch a drunk. In fact, Maylene had seen a mother pour alcohol down her son's throat once, just as a slug had got to him. The slippery red thing made an express exit out the back of his head, its burrowing mouth eager to be gone of the sodden body. Killed the boy in the process, but that was a mercy compared to what he would have become.

Maylene chased down bites of the aptly named hard tack with the dwindling supply of Dickel whiskey she'd picked up in Cougher's Bend. Only time in history it had paid to be a drunk, she thought.

Letting the alcohol burn away the hopelessness and dread, she unfurled her bedroll and tied the bandana tight around her nose and mouth.

* * *

Maylene felt a warm, wet wriggling at the corner of her mouth, and instantly surged awake, hands ripping at her face, pulling away the wet bandana, nerves afire. The bulbous, worm-like body pulsed in Maylene's fist, her cheek numb where the analgesic slime had done its work. Without another thought, she grabbed and twisted the slug with her other hand, pulling the thing apart in a spray of blood and a single high-pitched squeak. Blinking rapidly, she tried to get her cat eyes in the dark, only seeing smeary blurs of gray at first. Gradually, the desert slowly revealed itself in a dim wash of shapes.

"Raul?" she said into the pregnant, silent dark. No response.

Maylene looked down at the pale clay ground, and saw the shape of a body near the lip of the canyon. "*Raul!*" she hissed loudly. Nothing. "Goddamnit," she sighed, thinking the *bandito* had drunk himself into a stupor. She realized that she herself was no longer drunk, her head throbbing with a hangover.

Maylene knelt next to Raul and rolled him onto his back. Instantly, she felt his strong hands seizing and pulling her down, arms shooting out like the spring-loaded turd that waits in all jack-in-the-boxes. His eyes were all white, his mouth hanging open in a stupid O.

"Not you," she said, biting back tears, her one and only ally in this hell-world now one of them. Maylene saw two shapes wriggling towards her in the dark, burrowing out of the clay. *Raul was right*, she thought, *they do move slow in the cold*. They glacially inched up his ruler-straight arms, towards her. His hands were two fleshy vices, locked around her neck. She let go of his arms, it was no use. Trying to pry them loose was like trying to pry a boulder from the earth. Instead, Maylene pulled out her revolver. "I'll tell John you...weren't like the others," she croaked, throat going tight.

She stuck the thick barrel into Raul's gaping maw, aiming down so the bullet would exit through his neck, and closed her eyes as she pulled the trigger. Maylene felt one of his teeth ricochet off her forehead along with a few warm slaps of blood, the shout of her death-bringer ringing out across the world. The hands fell away, and the valley went quiet once more.

Mama's home, you slithering shits, Maylene thought bitterly, realizing the stealthy approach was useless, and in the end, liking it that way. She stomped the two encroaching slugs into slop, quickly rifling through the dead man's pockets, and not giving a hoot in Hell about any of it. Raul would've done the same.

She liberated his *bandolero* belt, and looped it around her own wiry frame, looking like a true bandito. Maylene added his Colt revolver, a slightly smaller model than the custom-made hand cannons she wore, as well as two sticks of dynamite, *of course*. She considered the half-bottle of *Soro*. Maylene fucking hated tequila, thought it tasted like cactus piss, but snatched it anyway, landing on the notion that beggars couldn't be choosers. *Not in this God-forsaken world*, she thought.

"Descansa tranquilo, amigo," she said to the dead man, pouring some tequila out in remembrance, then knocking back a slug herself. As the bitter booze seared her stomach, Maylene felt a black wave of rage flood her, knowing she was working herself up into a mean drunk. She got like this sometimes, and John had respected the curse of all redheaded women. *They don't call you fire-headed for nothin', sugar.*

With a mountain lion's grace, she slid down the side of the gulch, a red cloud blossoming behind her. As she came full on into the valley, the great cave loomed before her like a black gullet. No guards posted. *Damn shame*, she thought.

The mood to kill was on her now. Every kind soul those fuckin' worms had taken from the world had suddenly called her by name, and her jaw clenched, trigger fingers cramped with the urge to pull home.

Maylene strolled boldly into the cave, eyes blazing blue, cold fire with both hammers at full cock, a belly full of tequila sending her on a warpath.

* * *

They came in waves, sluggish at first. Armed sentries stared at her, their guns lowered, uninterested in ruining a perfectly good body. Instead, they just bolted awkwardly for her, trying to pin her down, and Maylene shot them mercilessly.

"Come on, you sumbitches!" she hollered drunkenly, aiming for their throats, not wasting time on the head or chest. Her cartridges were designed for maximum penetration power, the high-yield "slug hunter" rounds having nearly twice the powder charge of a normal cartridge. Every shot was meant to tear into the neck through cartilage and bone, shattering vertebrae and splitting the little nape-nested fuckers in half on the way out. The guns kicked like a surly draft horse, but she'd used them enough to know how to compensate for the massive recoil. Her guns spoke in a steady unceasing roar as the cavern acoustics grabbed her shots and stretched them out into something monstrous. She hoped the grubs heard those war drums of her destruction and cowered in their little mud holes.

"Where'd you put him, huh? *Where is he!*" Maylene screamed as she stomped onwards, the co-opted humans falling by the wayside and the exposed worms piling up. She'd made it about a quarter mile into the cave, having taken a torch off one of the poor vessels and holding her smoking gun in the other hand.

Maylene stopped abruptly as she came around a bend and looked up, movement drawing her eye. "What in...the Hell?" she said, almost panting, as she stared up at a ceiling lined with pale, gaunt faces.

Numbering in the hundreds, each of their bodies encased in a tawny chrysalis, a crop of human stalactites hung above her, married to the ceiling with that terrible glistening shell. She saw small cuts on each side of the throat, the feeding arteries of those imprisoned sliced open just enough for a steady, slow trickle. Men, women, children, all of their ethnicities and origins homogenized by the cigarette-ash pallor they shared. She watched as their prisons undulated, rhythmically squeezing the poor souls like a giant hand squeezing a lemon for its juice. Blood dripped and flowed from these hellish pupae, a gentle crimson rain whose droplets Maylene followed to the ground.

That's when she saw the channels, smooth little canals bored into the hard rock, all glistening and painted red, a deluge of human life flowing ever downwards.

"Sweet Jesus," Maylene said, swooning on her feet slightly. She took another swig of the *Soro* from her pack, not only needing to keep up inebriation as a defensive measure, but also to soften this abhorrent sight, this devil's wet dream.

A horrifying noise shocked her out of her haunted awe, like that of wet pasta on God's twirling spoon. Maylene watched more worms foaming up from of the soil, this lot bigger and more aggressive than any she'd ever seen. Unlike their smaller counterparts, these came at her with viper speed, biting at her where they could, then hissing and dropping away as they tasted her ethanol-tainted blood.

"Whassamatter, too tart for ya, fuckers?" Maylene yelled, ripping her knife from its place, and slashed at the fat red bodies. She marched through that scarlet storm, stomping on blood-gorged grubs as she went, looking for John's exposed face. They were alive, anemic and on the verge of death yes, but *alive*, she could see that by the shifting expressions of agony on their gaunt visages as they were milked. The grubs were keeping them alive somehow, the bloodletting slow and methodical, which meant there was a purpose to this nightmare. That meant John had to be alive, and just as the thought struck her, she saw him.

Barely recognizable, if not for the long crescent scar along his left eye. It had been a parting gift from a human trafficker down in Laredo who preferred the first option in the term "dead or alive".

"John!" she gasped, aiming for the small root-like aperture

that stuck them to the cave ceiling. The shot echoed off the walls as his cocoon fell, and Maylene dropped the torch to put out her hands out for him. She expected the big man's weight to knock her to the ground, but the lightness of him was terrible. It was like catching a grain sack. "Oh, John…" she sighed, looking at the blanched wheat of his once brown hair. Maylene gently placed him on the ground, cutting away the waxy carapace, revealing an emaciated, naked body. Tears sprung to her eyes at the once mighty frame reduced to twigs and sinew.

"Ma…Maylene?" His glazed-over eyes took her in from a place beyond comprehension.

"I'm here, honey..," she gasped, taking out her waterskin. Only a few swallows left. Her husband's chapped lips closed around the tip and sucked, his slender throat bobbing. More worms came, and she slashed at them with small, indignant cries. "*Get the fuck away from him!*" Maylene screamed, her blade sundering and slicing, the other arm protectively around her love.

"Maylene…listen to me," John rasped in a fragile voice, sounding as raw as he looked. She leaned close, holding him. "You gotta…finish her, Maylene. The Queen."

"Huh? What're you—"

"She's down there…been feeding her. It all leads back there. Kill her…and you'll kill them. It's what I… I'd been trying to find this whole time..," he said, the words squeaking around something hard in what remained of his throat.

"I can't leave you, we gotta get out of here, we—"

He grabbed for Raul's Colt, and she marveled that even in his sorry state, he could tell which gun wasn't hers.

"I can still shoot," John said with a weak smile. "Go down there…*finish* this. Or all of *this*—" He gestured towards the ceiling with its hellish human décor, "Will never end. Ever."

Even as he spoke, Maylene saw the worms were getting desperate, burrowing into their suspended food supply and co-opting the weak bodies. The chrysalides excreted them the way a farmer's hands would squeeze a plump udder for its milk. They fell to the ground in a heap, slowly crawling towards the reunited lovers, emaciated bodies struggling to cooperate with their rider's commands.

"Go, Maylene. *Go,*" John insisted.

Against all her instincts, she did. She left him with the Soro, not sure if alcohol would kill him in his current state, cinched the ammo belt around him, and headed downwards. As she descended, the concentration of hanging bodies above her increased, every crimson droplet across her shoulders becoming the seed of a downpour.

* * *

Maylene had lost track of how long she'd had to walk. She was deep underground, the slope of the cavern floor growing steeper as she went, boots slipping in blood that slicked every inch of the stone floor.

The ceiling of the narrow tunnel she'd been following moaned with a hundred mouths, imprisoned but not quite dead. She trudged on, beneath that choir of the damned, until the passage abruptly opened up into a vast atrium.

"My God..." Maylene said, soaked red from head to toe, having followed the river of blood to its headwaters.

There were three of them, each the size of a small wagon. Their bodies throbbed in time to some unseen heartbeat, their plump red carapaces lined with dozens of prolapsed sphincters that shat out a continuous stream of red riders. *The source,* she thought. John was right.

The worms all moved in hypnotizing murmuration, like wingless red starlings, headed towards Maylene with singular purpose.

She thought of Raul as she took out the two sticks of dynamite, full charge ones meant to blast through bedrock. Despite her horrible blood-soaking, the book of kitchen matches had kept dry in the inner pocket of her duster. Maylene struck one and took it to the whole pack, which went up with a *whoosh*. The green fuses were each five inches long, providing about thirty seconds of haul-ass time. She lit both, knowing once lit, nothing could put them out.

"Fuck you. Fuck every single last one of you, and your mothers," Maylene said, tossing the sizzling sticks into the bulbous mass before her. She ran, the surging tide of crimson leeches a biblical thing at her heels, but she was quicker. Moments later, the only thing that existed was a thunder that liked to have split her head open, the light of a thousand suns, and the pillars of Hell falling down behind her scrambling feet.

* * *

Part of her wanted to rescue them all, but she had seen what John had become. It was hopeless. They wouldn't have time to marshal all those weak, emaciated bodies out of the cave before the man-made tumult closed the door forever. In a desperate bid to stop her, the worms had wriggled through and piloted some of the wasted bodies under their power. By the time she reached him, John had put two down and was fending off three more, his gun hand still true despite its trembling.

Maylene scooped him up like a sack of potatoes, but knew they had no chance. Least she could do was put an end to their suffering, meaning true death for them all, and as the cavern came down behind her, she hoped she had accomplished just that. John continued to spit lead from over her shoulder, watching the cave swallow itself hole. She heard the metallic click of her husband's iron firing long after the gun was empty, long after they were clear of the Gulch. John would have never let them take him alive again.

Maylene put her wet cheek across his neck, knowing full well she wouldn't have, either.

* * *

They travelled for two days without stopping. The goddamned donkey slowed to a crawl as if to spite Maylene, and her audacity to increase its burden with another body, but they encountered no red riders. No bandits. Desolation embraced them, and they threw their arms around it gladly. Eventually, civilization materialized from that adobe hell, and Maylene had gotten them a room at a boarding house in one of the few border towns still alive with commerce and wealth, Gentry's Bend. She herself was covered from head to toe in red crust, looking like some kind of swamp hag from the belly of hell, and the man was a bag of bones at her feet. Despite their sorry condition, folks recognized the married-law couple, and Miss Gentry herself gave them room and board for free.

Maylene stayed in that room for over a week, slowly nursing her husband back to health, and taking heavy to the Dickell while she did so, trying to blot out what she saw in those caves. She thought if she had done all that for nothing, her mind would eat itself. At that point, a bullet in his head would be a blessing, and the one she'd put into her own would be a prayer. The wife of John Baker would have castrated the Devil himself with a square spoon before she'd let the riders get to them.

But one day, Maylene long lost track of the number of times the sun crawled across the sky in her whiskey stupor, Miss Gentry came to her.

"You heard the news?" she asked.

"Huh?" Maylene said. She was laying on the bed next to John, spoon feeding him beef broth. His color had come back, and some of that leather-lean disposition of his, but he was still weak as a kitten.

"Come look. Apparently, it's been like this all over," Gentry said, ushering her downstairs.

"I'll be back, don't go makin' a mess now," Maylene said, kissing a forehead that radiated a febrile heat.

"Say I do, that mean I get a sponge bath?" John asked, his voice still raw, but the smile that pulled up his lips in the corners showed he was getting some of his piss and vinegar back.

Maylene shook her head, tears pushing at her eyes, and a surge of love swelling her heart. God, how she hoped they could bring the world back to how it used to be. It sure as Hell wasn't perfect before, but it was a damn sight better than the nightmare the worms had turned it into.

She followed Miss Gentry outside, where a crowd had formed around the main thoroughfare, and shouldered up to see what all the commotion was.

"They stumbled into town, sorta shamblin' around aimlessly, then just collapsed," Miss Gentry said, pointing at the men. They wriggled on the ground as if the parasites inside them had forgotten how to pilot their cherished vessels.

One shuddered violently, arched his back at a spine-cracking angle, then shuddered some more as the back of his head bulged. A fat red worm oozed out from the nape of his neck and moved sluggishly along the adobe. They all watched silently to see what it would do. Instead of making a bee-line for the nearest walking, talking piece of meat, it just kept winding around in circles. It was moving the way a thing should when it has no spine and lives in the dirt.

"Lost their queen, now they don't know what to do," Maylene observed, rubbing her arms at a sudden chill in the air. Winter was coming, their first since the red rider scourge had begun. Raul had said they slow down in the cold, and she hoped the combination of the empty throne and the coming snowy wastes would be the death blow.

Maylene watched as the corpulent red abomination shriveled up like a sun dried coyote turd, and allowed herself to hope.

After everything, she could dare that much.

IT COMES FOR US ALL(CO-WRITTEN WITH KOREY DAWSON)

The sky was hemorrhaging around them.

A deep red spread from the east as the sun retreated behind the jagged peaks, the once vivid blue day dying, bleeding out into night. The landscape was so great and barren, no sound dared emanate from it.

When the two men started their palaver, the silence was so thick, it was as if the desert were leaning in to listen.

“Water,” the man on the ground said.

“So thirst touches you,” Sho’keh said, handing over the bladder. “Blanket women say bullets slide around you like snails on a cowpatty.”

“They say a lot of things, paintface. The bullets..,” Tom Dallion said, tipping it to his cracked lips, “They touch me.”

The bounty hunter touched his hip, a cloud of dust rising from the wing of his coat.

“I could see your blood with this.”

Dallion sneered. “Untie me, reckon you’d likely find out.”

Sho’keh shook his head, a rare curl of a smile touching his

lips. "No money."

At this, the white man made like a donkey and brayed. Laughed so hard his Stetson fell off. In the glow of the fire, one could make out the fine down of those few hairs that still clung to the pink scalp with dogged determination.

"Shit boy, that's a good'n," the older man said, getting up with a grunt. His walk wasn't quite a limp, but even with the slack of rope, it was enough to tell in his gait which leg he favored. "Got half a mind to test you. How fast you git up 'n go with that iron?"

Around them, saguaro cacti sprouted up from the unending sand pan like stoic sentries of this dry and deadly hellscape. He pointed his tied hands out to one of these green acts of floral defiance, in particular one that stood taller than the others, its twin arms curving upwards like a man in defeat.

"Say that out there was me. Middle stem muh noggin, other two muh arms, like sayin 'I surrender!'" Dallion said.

Sho'keh sat across the fire with his hands in his lap, legs crossed over each other. His face was like a bronze dish holding a pair of hot coals.

"I'll even say it," the white man said, sharp hazel eyes never leaving the cactus. "I surrender." He jutted his flat jaw towards the bounty hunter, as if inviting him to take a swing. "Just humor me, boy."

The man looked at his captive like a child, and sighed, looking back towards the horse.

"I surren—"

Before his captive could blink, the bounty hunter's arm moved in a blur, a smooth synchronistic motion with the swivel of his torso, as the revolver was out and cracking thunder across the desert. Three times, three thunderclaps, all in the space of a breath. His scarred hand still extended the shooting iron as it smoked. A gun that looked like it weighed as much as a wagon wheel, held out as easily as a struck match.

Despite the fading light, they both could see the exploded branches of the cactus, glowing with fire. It had happened faster than a string of firecrackers in the hearth. Smooth as you please, the big gun was back in its holster, bleeding the last of its smoke across the Indian's ribs.

"Well, now I know how quick you'd drop a Christian," Dallion said, ears ringing. "If one had a mind to skedaddle, that is."

Sho'keh turned a stick in the base of the fire, annoying it into greater fury.

"Savage wouldn't even give a man on the run chance to change his mind," the white man said to himself. His smile was a thin, humorless line. "Wouldn't matter how many times you shot me. Bullets touch me...they just don't hurt," the captive said. Another bray of laughter as he awkwardly picked his Stetson up.

As Dallion poked a finger through a hole by the hatband, the bounty hunter brought out something from the pocket of his jacket. He moved the gold star in his fingers, glinting in the firelight, the words New Mexico engraved around its center.

"My people," Sho'keh said, indicating the star, "My fathers would have honored this. Yours marked you with it." The bounty hunter drew a thumb from the left side of his neck to his armpit, and coughed. "Your black heart, stained this forever."

"Man of honor, huh? Yeah, we'll see how clean you are when you're standing in front of the ones with the money," Dallion said, "Just as likely to plant your red ass as me."

The older man managed to sit the hat back on his balding pate, and flopped down on a blanched piece of log. "Word of advice, I would fast the day before. You don't wanna die with your britches full. Speaking of which, ahh...suppertime, " Dallion said, as his captor took the two smoking skewers that'd been cooking off the fire. The viper's flayed body almost resembled a long sausage, its browned flesh curling.

"Eat," the bounty hunter said, holding a skewer under the

man's face. "The mule need not carry a dead man."

Dallion's trail-worn visage crinkled up in disgust. "I don't want that burned turd. I need *fresh* meat...still bleeding," the white man said.

Sho'keh ripped a bite off the cooked snake, then reached back, offering the skewer he had kept for himself. "Come on, fell-ah," the bounty hunter said, affecting something of his captive's accent. "Gotta eat. You starve, no pay. *Take* it." In a flash, Dallion snatched the skewer with his teeth and ripped it from the leathery hand, flinging as far into the desert as he could.

"I said, I ain't *eatin'* that shit."

The bounty hunter took a second mouthful of snake. "Empty belly on trail, then you get rope for your neck. Pain behind you, pain ahead of you," Sho'kay said, holding out the remains on his skewer. "You've eaten your own. Eat this today."

"Nothing can kill me," Dallion said, pointing both thumbs at one temple, "While it's here. Get up real close, and you'll see...just you step across."

Sho'keh stepped past the man in the ruined Stetson to find the rejected meal. "No need to shoot you. Only mercy you want, is from gallows."

"Lift my shirt," the captive said.

The bounty hunter made a quick sound, somewhere between a hiccup and a snort.

"I been peppered up like a two-bit steak in my time. You don't believe? I'll show you," he said, motioning with his chin towards the thin, long sleeved shirt he had on. Ropy muscle could be seen through the thin fabric. "Go on. I won't bite," Dallion said, grinning.

There were some that still called Sho'keh savage, but no one called him stupid. He'd survived by making his life, true to his way, in blood and life abundant. When a contingent of militia offered a truce to his people on the strength of his tracking and scoutcraft, he learned how to move among other animals. Returning from that duty with their tongue across his lips, painted by Great Father, but still forgotten, he hunted men. It hadn't been stupidity that had let him survive 32 years.

Still, curiosity pulled at him. Sho'keh took a long stick and, keeping an arm's length from the man, pushed up the shirt. His jaw bulged with a wad of tough snake flesh, his other hand already holding the Colt.

Sho'keh took in the sight before him, his eyebrows crushed together in disbelief. His captive's fish-belly white flesh was marred and puckered, looking like the surface of the moon on nights it hung pregnant and shining in the sky. The older man looked like he'd been shot and knitted up at least two dozen times. The mountainous scar tissue extended up into the torso and disappeared under the shirt.

He had seen many strange things in his young life, but took a cautionary step back at this. It was something more from the skin-house, a ghost on legs, skittering around the edges of his sweating vision, that time of death horses screaming and hawks flying in his face without their feathers to know them. The white man now grinned like a loon, a wet sprig of hair falling over one eye as his hat pitched to the side in his laughter.

"So sally on, hunter. Open me up like that cactus. It'll be on *you* then," Dallion said, "And by its eyes and deeds, you...you'll know Hell."

That night, he looked down at the strange, disgraced man, and tied an extra layer of knots in his restraints. Tied him like a hog crazy with worms, and still he felt it wasn't enough. He kept the fire burning high, one of his shooting irons laying half out of its holster, ready to slip out like butter in a hot skillet if the man, fallen from the white law, moved.

He kept still, but couldn't find sleep. The scars pushed at his mind, the litany of them speaking to bodily devastation far beyond what any human could withstand. Sho'keh thought of the many aberrations that existed in the dark of this world, and those he had encountered himself. Just behind the walls and wheels of the civilized men, things still *moved.* Things they would know to be unnatural, and what he saw here at his feet, what had *radiated* off this man like the stink of a gangrenous limb, was an unnaturalness of the highest order.

It'll be on you then, the white man had said.

* * *

They entered the town of Socorro the next day, having ridden six hours across more unending brown. Upon entering the small desert town, which hugged the Rio Grande and was really only a smattering of shotgun shacks and a few places of commerce, they seemed to have drawn the attention of every mutt, stray and claimed.

"Got damn, these dogs must smell the bullshit in yuh," Dallion said, doing his best to navigate his bound carcass away from the snarling, jumping throng of canines, his mule braying at their tenacity. Sho'keh attempted to calm his horse, tugged this way and that by the frantic movement of the pack animal leashed to it. The *thunk* of a hoof in the snout, a yelp, then calm.

"They can smell the dead," the bounty hunter said. As the snarls turned into whines, he looked back. Sho'keh saw his captive baring his teeth at the pack, then heard a loud *clack clack clack* as he tapped his jaws together violently. The horrible noise seemed to hold within it some harbinger of death for them, and the mutts scrambled, tail tucked as if a warning shot had just been fired. Despite the hot sun intent on boiling him alive under his coat, the sight of that odd exchange chilled him. Sho'keh knew an ancient and primal establishment of the pecking order when he saw it.

"Let's go, you flathead sumbitch," Dallion said, "Times a'wastin' and you're taking me exactly where I want to go."

Sho'keh spurred his horse into a canter as they rode through town, drawing stares from Socorro's mix of whites, Indians, and Spaniards alike.

* * *

"Lookie pa! Someone's ridin' in with a prisoner!" The bounty hunter heard the boy's voice from inside the store as he tied up the horses and his luggage, looking up at the sign. *Socorro Crossroads Supplies and Sundries,* it read. As Sho'keh entered, a man sprang up from behind the counter, a pencil behind one ear. He blinked as if he were an apparition.

"You're a long way from home, mister. This is a town of the New Mexico territories," the man said flatly, as the owner of the boyish voice showed himself. The kid had a mop of brown hair slicked back into a ducktail just like his daddy, and his eyes looked about to fall out of his head.

"I know where I'm at," Sho'keh said, "But I need to get where I'm going." He approached the counter, unrolling a two-foot map showing a magnified view of the Tri-State Territories. "Albuquerque. Somewhere around here now...need to get to *here,*" the bounty hunter said, a wide finger moving across to the star.

"Hey mister, how many scalps you take on the Bozeman trail?"

"Cut a cross for Colonel Shelby, my friend, and buried him," Sko'keh said coldly, "Never cut no scalps. I'm bound for Albuquerque." He watched the cashier point his finger about four inches south of where he had estimated he was.

"You're all mixed up, fella. You're farther away than you think...some folks don't take, well... Gotta follow the Rio Grande —"

"Ya been south of the border, ever stick any *banditos* down yonder?"

“Hush now, Joseph, trying to see this...gentleman on his way,” the cashier said impatiently. The bounty hunter felt his breakfast of cured pork and whisky percolate uncomfortably in his gut at the boy’s incessant interrogation. He knew that the reputation of “walking braves”, mysterious and cantankerous hellions who traded feathers for dungarees and killed for argument and drink, wasn’t without merit. Sho’keh had never stooped to be one of those ornery “shoot first and ask later” trackers, playing fast and loose with the boundaries of ethics and cruelty, but he did put bloody coin in his pocket from time to time. Now he was just trying to make an honest dollar and keep his hide intact in the process.

“What you do is, you follow the Rio Grande up, bout twenty five miles. You’re gonna hook across at Las Lunas, Spanish feller there who’ll get you cross the river with a ferry. From there it’s a straight shot north for another twenty. Bad country up that way though, if I’m to speak frank,” the cashier said.

“Born and raised in bad country,” Sho’keh said, looking at the boy, instead of his father. “Not on *roads.*”

The boy pointed towards the donkey’s bound rider. “He a *bad* man?”

“Bad man,” the bounty hunter said, picking supplies off the shelf. Jarred preserves, salt, a bottle of whiskey. The boy followed him around like a shadow.

“He kill people?”

“Many.” Sho’keh took his wares up to the counter. He took a piece of stamped stationary from his pocket and a small nub of pencil.

“That feller looks like an Indian,” a toothless old man in a chair near a far window said to himself, rocking. The boy looked towards the man as his pa counted up the items. “Looks that way, don’t it, Felton?”he said, almost shouting.

The bounty hunter inwardly winced at the price, and slid

the paper to the cashier. "Notary stamped this for expenses, to pursue bounty. Seven dollars, fifty seven cents," Sho'kah said, writing out the price and signing with his official name. The cashier carefully scrutinized the paper.

"Recovery Agent Joseph...hey, son," the clerk said, "Y'all have the same name!"

A strange look came across the boy's face like someone had stepped over his grave, but had left a gold bar behind instead of a bouquet.

"Recovery Agent Joseph Thorn-in-lip, dispatched from... under Franklin...Bail Bondsman...Bernalillo County..." He read the form like he was announcing a death in the family. "Well, listen here, Agent Thorn-in-lip. That Spanish feller up the way don't take no IOU. He'll just as soon dump your ass in the river. Now I ain't gonna cause no fuss, that shootin' iron looks like it could take the hump off a buffalo, and you've caused enough trouble just walkin' in. But I better be hearin' from this *Franklin* gentleman pretty soon," the cashier said, his voice going tight as he tried to be brave.

"You will," Sho'keh said, making his way out the store, items in hand. The boy followed him outside as he loaded his saddlebags.

"Why's he gotta go all the way up north? What's in Albuquerque? Why not just shoot him dead, pow!" the boy said, leveling an imaginary revolver at the bound man, who stared impassively into the air, as if contemplating life's great mysteries.

"Killing was in New Mexico, he hid in Texas. Found him there, taking him back. Alive...they pay more," Sho'keh said, untethering his horse.

"It true, mister? You kill some people up in 'Querque?" the boy asked as he mounted, and they began a slow trot through the thoroughfare.

"Yep. Ate em, too," Dallion said, in a conversational tone.

* * *

Sho'keh shifted in his saddle, remembering the leather seat outside Franklin's office, top button cinched as he had walked in as Joseph Thorn-in-lip. An alienist of the bondsman's acquaintance had visited the office to get a dossier put together if, once captured, he would find himself interviewing Dallion. The voices hummed through the glass as he waited.

"Why'd he go and eat them folks, huh, doc? Why not just kill em and be on his way?"

"It's just in his nature."

"The hell that even mean? Ain't in a man's nature to eat another man."

"The party from Illinois that found themselves snowbound in the Sierras...they were placed in circumstances beyond their control. In this case, he controlled the circumstances himself. He may even be in a class that ceases to be classified as a man."

"He's a *man*," Franklin grunted. "Just a man that's...nuttier than a pecan pie filled with squirrel turds."

Neither man spoke at that, then the door had opened, and Sho'keh had stepped aside to allow the waddling little man out as he entered. The next thing in his path had been the hunt.

* * *

The fire crackled in the silence and Sho'keh's jaw muscles bunched as he forced a bite of hard tack down. Dallion still wouldn't eat, four days he'd been in the bounty hunter's charge, and hadn't eaten so much as a crumb. Yet, he looked none the worse for wear.

"The hell they call you where you from anyway? Did you

earn a name in your tribe?"

"Two-Times Mother saw baby smacking thistle from his face. Thorn-in-lip, she said. On the line of your paper, in the Territories, Joseph Thorn-in-lip."

"But that's not your name..," Dallion said, face cracked in half, all teeth. "Is it, now?"

The bounty hunter set his jaw, a cliff face against the firelight. "Sho'keh."

"Shoky? Shokha? Sounds like you're tryna cough up a hairball. I'm just gonna call you Shithead. That's close enough."

"Won't say it long, so...close enough," Sho'keh agreed.

* * *

Indeed, the Spanish feller did not kin to IOU's. From the language that he knew, Javier Ibanez had told Sho'keh that he could either pay up, or him and his hog tied *gringo* could piss up a rope.

There was a queue of people waiting to get on the ferry, a log barge that looked like it could hold 15-20 people. As the bounty hunter struggled to come to a compromise, offering the surly Spaniard everything from the half bottle of Ten High he'd gotten in Saccuro to the turquoise belt buckle around his waist, he'd heard a commotion going on behind him. An old voice shouting in some agitated native tongue. He knew Apache and Pawnee from his time before the militia, but whatever was being spoken was neither of those.

Sho'keh cast a glance back towards his horse, and saw an old woman haranguing Tom Dallion. Judging by her ceremonial shawl, she was native to the Plains as well, so he turned back to Javier, who was growing red faced.

"Mierda! Look what you are doing, fucking Indian pissing

off customers. Either pay or *Viete a la Mierde*!" the man shouted. The woman was growing increasingly emphatic with her words and gestures. A small crowd was drawing to observe this one sided argument and Sho'kah felt a cloud of tension thickening around him. He needed to break away.

"Here." the bounty hunter said, and with great reluctance, took a sweat-stained handkerchief from his pocket, and unwrapped the gold medallion from it. "Gold, solid gold. You comprende?" he said, not knowing if it was true, but shoving the Ranger's sigil into the brown hands all the same. If its function meant nothing to Dallion, its form meant less than nothing to him. He wiped his hands on his jacket, as if to move the stain of it to something else. As Javier examined the gold star, he nodded at Dallion, whose normal vacuous stare had turned sour.

"Alright now, what'd he do?" he said, trying to placate the old woman. She looked at the white man and then back at Sho'keh.

"This man prisoner?" she asked, her voice heavily accented.

Sho'keh leaned down to her, whispering in a tongue unknown to Javier.

"What's that?" Javier said, kicking a plume of dirt toward the prisoner, the mule blinking.

"My prisoner," Sho'keh said, turning to Javier. "Wanted for taking life, other crimes." The bounty hunter attempted to blur the facts to avoid being overtaken by the forming mob.

"This man *monster*. He need die. He need die!" she said, and then switched back to whatever tongue she hurled at Dallion.

"Ma'am, go easy now," the bounty hunter said, employing a phrase he had heard from Franklin's mouth. "He hunted outside of your people, you say men have talked of him?"

"No, I *smell it* on him! Sho'keh, please!" she yelled. The bounty hunter felt his bowels loosen as she said his name, he thought himself invisible in these towns. "*Kill* him!"

Before he could respond, she was thrusting a small burlap pouch into his hands.

"Use this. You kill him!" she said, pointing a gnarled, arthritic finger at Dallion.

"*Madre de dios,* man, what he do, shit on her ancestors?" Javier said. "Come on, before you scare all my customers away." He was holding the medallion with a satisfied look on his face, the edge of the gold star indented with bite marks. It apparently passed muster for the ferryman. Eager to be gone of this woman and her pleas, Sho'keh pulled the reins of his horse and led his sorry entourage onto the ferry.

All but Sho'keh, his captive, and three others declined to ride, looking at Dallion like he might turn into something biblical and kill them all. As they made their way down the swirling Rio, the bounty hunter peered inside the small sack. He stared for a long time, remembering the fetish bags his weathered elders wore. As he walked among the civilized peoples, he waved off such native hoodoo in their faces, but he still remembered the wrinkled man.

Fish-Ears, big medicine. Sho'keh had watched him spread his hands against a thick mist when a morning raid had woke them from their skins. The shroud lifted back, the figures plain to see, like shadows with tomahawk hands running across a white blanket. Fish-Ears stood before the children, still unseen in the haze around only him. The men had let fly, the raiding party as quilled as porcupines, steaming on the ground.

Since then, he'd had made it a rule of life to listen to wise old folks, native or otherwise, who had a thing to say on a matter he was involved in.

"What'd she give you? Smells like shit," the disgraced lawman said.

Sho'keh felt something cold in his gut at this. He been standing some five feet away, and the man had spoken as if he was right next to him,

"No business of yours," the bounty hunter said, unnerved. *Something under his skin,* Fish-Ears said in his mind, *double ugly, toad feet.* He closed the sack and put it in his breast pocket. For the next hour or so, his mind turned and turned, trying to put the pieces together.

* * *

"Albuquerque, two days ride. *Yo que tou,* I try make it in one. Full moon come out tonight. Brings out crazy. Wicked men between here and there," Javier told his passengers as he tied off the barge to the dock. Sho'keh raised his hand to him as he guided his horse, mule and Dallion off the dock and onto solid land. Blasted tan and brown was now blasted brown and red, adobe coloring the ground in crimson, the sun crawling across the sky like a wounded animal trying to find cover behind the mountains.

Sho'keh felt a strong sense of urgency then. He judged he had some four hours to ride before night was upon them. Things swarmed in his head as he stared at the white man draped across the mule. The night was no longer alone. It was if his one body contained a multitude of crawling, orgiastic shapes, and they had started marching around the horses like a fire dance on the last day of the world. The contents of the sack, the woman's dire pleading, Javier's comment about the moon...Sho'keh felt invisible, icy fingers playing across the nape of his neck. His balls receded deep into his body, as if a bear had ripped off the top of his tent like the lid of a pot. Then, nothing of what he had felt remained, except for a metallic taste on his tongue. It hadn't come from inside...blood was in the air.

He opened his eyes, unassuming open desert looming before him, vast and empty. Sho'kah couldn't explain what was around him, but looked over at the mule, and unexpectedly, into the staring eyes of his captive. Dallion's eyes shone in the moonlight, somehow moving in the stillness of his smiling face, like silver coins in the bottom of a disturbed well.

* * *

Right as dusk had begun to discolor the sky, Sho'keh noticed Dallion was looking a might peaked. The man's chalky complexion had gotten positively transparent, his skin oiled with sweat. Not only that, his horse had grown awful skittish, the way she did after hearing a gunshot, or on the rare occasion when a cougar took to stalking them. The mule was none too happy either, making disgruntled noises to accompany the horse's protestations. Tension pulled Sho'keh's nerves taught, as though an invisible hook had caught in his neck and connected to his asshole, the unseen fisherman pulling hard.

They stopped at the lip of a large valley, the Rio Grande to their right, the land festooned with shallow arroyos ahead.

"Should have eaten, your belly is eating you," he told Dallion as he helped him off the mule. Sho'keh saw the veins and chords of his neck standing out, like he was in the throes of passing a kidney stone or a particularly large bowel movement.

"Be a lot better if you untied me," Dallion said, his voice strained.

"My blood's mostly whisky," Sho'keh said, stacking kindling with the hint of a smile. "Almost home. One more night, then you can die." He unfurled his bed roll, taking his time clearing the ground with his boot to weed out any scorpions or snakes.

Satisfied, he struck flint to steel and the dry wood he collected erupted into flames. As it blazed, he poured the contents of the bag into his palm, the silver image glinting in the firelight.

"The hell is that?" Dallion asked. The white man had been cool, even apathetic since he had been picked up. For the first time since Laredo, Sho'keh heard weakness in his voice.

The bounty hunter walked towards him, extending a closed fist.

Dallion tried to snicker, but coughed instead, a dark spittle leaking onto his cheek.

"Sure saw *this* comin' over the fence," he said. "Well, come on ahead, then, Shithead. Had my licks before and reckon I won't put up a fuss-"

Sho'keh opened his fist in front of Tom Dallion's face, the silver necklace dropping on its chain, a gleaming bolt of white from the sun and fire. The change in the bound man was instantaneous. Dallion raked violently at his face with the rope at his wrists, his eyes rolled over white, lids fluttering. The bindings strained under his kicking legs, chest heaving in a blur like to crack his ribs. Sho'keh almost stepped back into the fire, but righted himself, if only to see the outcome. He heard a muscular grinding sound as Dallion's jaw opened too wide for a snake, much less a man. A net of pulsing black veins had branched across his face, and somehow, hair began to sprout and run down onto his forehead, like a melting candle. His eyes snapped back to focus, the entire framework then falling to a heap from what must have been a foot off the earth.

Sho'keh knelt down next to his quarry, holding the charms to fog over in front of his nose. It could have been the photograph he had been shown before he left Franklin's office. He was looking down at the figure of Thomas Dallion, formerly of the New Mexico Rangers, no longer the disgraced lawman and cannibal of his bounty papers. Draping the necklace around the man's neck, he thought of gods and what they do.

* * *

The smell of musk and cooking meat was in the air as the bounty hunter looked across the fire at a man he had ridden with for miles, but now could barely recognize.

Dallion was sitting up straight as if he was leaning against wallboard, his collar shot, the face above it a mask of confusion. "Like to trouble you for a nip, if you could spare't."

Sho'keh took a tin cup from next to the water pot and poured in a finger of Ten High, then reached to the man, forcing him to lean towards the fire. The cluster of charms swung from his neck like a pendulum as he took the cup. A rudely shaped silver *milagro,* Santa Lucia with two eyeballs in a tray, crossed swords at her neck. The expected wooden crucifix, with small rough-hewn metal spikes inlaid. Clinking against them both, a strange jar no bigger than a cork contained the ashy remains of a black moth, crushed to fit.

Dallion winced, drawing from the cup much too slowly. "Where'd ya pick me up? Got me fettered cozy, much better than I ever done to a man."

"Laredo," the bounty hunter said, turning the meat in the fire. Dallion had slept as still as a corpse, long enough for Sho'keh to stick a young musk pig on the run. Now, looking at the emaciated Ranger, he wondered whether it smelled akin to man flesh.

"Better'n forty score out from home, and how many years," he said, picking up the folded Weekly Citizen his captor had given him upon waking, "Them boys from White Oaks, and the panhandlers, the camp at Wingate, Judge Maitland...my wife. Not Bill...and little Bonnie. Not *them*, as well?"

"And more besides," Sho'keh said, raising his own drink.

Dallion flung the paper, grasping his wailing mouth with his hands. He crumpled in on himself, face cracked with sorrow. There wasn't enough water left in his body for tears.

"God help me," he said, reaching down for the necklace, "Please save this-" The moment his fingers touched the Santa Lucia, he clenched hard enough to break a tooth, blood popping out on his cheeks like the seeds of a strawberry. He wrenched loose, screaming and holding up his red hands to the firelight. “That bastard Hoyle did this! *Damned me!*”

Sho’keh reached to the knife propped against the coals. “You damned yourself. The sun’s turned over in its sleep too many times to pray for you. To *anyone*.”

The prisoner looked at him from under his scabby eyelids. “If my legs wouldn’t snap off under me, I’d jump on you,” Dallion said, his rabid look sinking as he spoke. “Make it so you lay my neck open with that pigsticker, see my Margaret, my…*little ones* again.”

The bounty hunter put the blade back in its place, and tossed one of the sticks of meat in front of Dallion. “No good,” he said, taking one for himself, “The dog-shape has been at your heels since Las Cruces, but Death no longer knows your name.”

Sho’keh took a bite of his own, pointing to his chest. “Atasaya,” he said.

Dallion’s eyes went wide. “When I caught hold of ‘im at Isleta Pueblo,” he said. “Hoyle was desert-crazy, paid some farmer’s sons to brand ‘im, right here.” The white man held two crossed fingers against the bridge of his nose. “Eyes blazed up, damn near ripped my head off my neck…put him down before he reached the Mission. Leaned over ‘im for some last reckonin’, he told me that Death would forget me, then died hisself.”

Sho’keh got to his feet, brushing his hands together.

“The place must have caught fire, because after that, all I could breath was smoke, and it felt like my clothes were burning,” Dallion said, growing louder, almost begging. “Then, I was here, hog-tied, with *you* drippin’ water across my cheeks.”

The bounty hunter left him and went to his horse, retrieving the muzzleloader he used as a deer rifle when they ran low on provisions. He brought the rifle back towards the fire, took out his powder funnel and stared at the silver talisman on the white man’s chest. Sho’keh poured a full charge down into the long octagonal barrel, looking in his prisoner's face.

"Wouldn't blame you for it, if you brushed me right here," Dallion said, "Reckon I'm only above snakes 'cause you put this here bauble on me."

The bounty hunter made a small movement, like a horse shooing a fly. "Saw a fire out there. This isn't for you," he said, pausing in his work. "Yet."

By the time Sho'keh had finished loading the rifle, his charge's condition had worsened considerably. The sun was finally receding behind the mountains, and hot on its tail was the moon, first coming small but then growing bigger and redder in the sky. It was going to be a blood moon tonight. As the moon grew from the size of a dinner plate to a wagon wheel in the sky, its pocked and cratered surface in breathtaking view, Sho' keh felt that charging of the atmosphere again. Both horse and mule were thoroughly perturbed, pulling at their moorings, and kicking up adobe.

"Don't owe me...nothin'," the white man said through his teeth, wet and shivering, "But he was headin' for a place...couldn't reckon why, after what he'd been doin'. San...Agustin...de la Isleta, mission in...the Pueblo."

Dallion was breathing heavy now, his eyes were half lidded and he started to rant in a tongue that sounded like a cougar drowning in hot mud. Kneeling down by the sick man, the bounty hunter watched as the older man's muscles bulged and slithered beneath the flesh like snakes. His jaundiced eyes locked an iron gaze on his captor.

"Reckon I know...why Hoyle went...there," he said. "Shoan... what's it?"

"Sho'keh," the bounty hunter said. "They say I cross the lake instead of walking around it, like you, wolf-brother."

Dallion gasped, gnashed his teeth at his captor. They looked wrong to be in that mouth, too many. Every time his head whipped around, it seemed as if more were there, like a flower opening with jagged petals. Sho'keh offered the man a sip of water from his canteen when he noticed the sound of hooves under the noises coming from Dallion's throat and gut.

"Banditos," the bounty hunter hissed as he stood, shooting irons out. His eyes looked around wildly as he tried to get a bead on the riders, and saw the thick plume of dust coming at them from just ahead. He heard laughs and a few gun shots as the riders intentionally made their presence known. A moment later, he got a look at the riders in the campfire's glow. They wore matching black dusters, their faces occulted by bandanas, the three of them holding firearms of various make and model.

"Well now, what do we have here?" the front most rider said, looking down at Sho'keh and the man at his feet. The bounty hunter drew back both hammers, the clicks loud and metallic.

"Recovery Agent. Bonded to take this prisoner to Bernalillo County. Don't care who you are, best be on your way," he said, in his Joe Thorn-in-lip voice. Dallion gave a low throaty groan by way of introducing himself.

"*Agent? Prisoner?*" the lead man said, like an old biddie with her teeth in the town gossip. "How exciting...I don't see no badge on you, *pendejo,*" he spat, saying this last like it was covered in dog shit.

Dallion was thrashing . "Gonna kill...all you," he growled. Sho'keh turned and saw the white man thrashing against his restraints. There was a squeaking sound of rope being pulled to its snapping point, and the bounty hunter looked at his prisoner's chest. The necklace was gone.

"That fella don't look so good. He got a price on his head?" one of the other riders asked.

"There's gonna be a bullet in yours, you don't mosey on outta here," Sho'keh said, the fishhook in his neck pulling hard now, and saw the eyes of the head rider widen.

"The hell is... wrong with him?" he said. Sho'keh didn't take his eyes off the rider's hands, but heard something inhuman emanating from the ground. Just then, the banditos' horses spooked, many rearing up and shucking off their human cargo. The bounty hunter whipped around and watched a metamorphosis overcame Dallion.

His body seemed to swell with new muscle, changing shape, his legs and arms lengthening, the audible crackle and crunch of bones moving and rearranging within the body. He let out a yell mingled with something akin to a screech owl, and his whole body trembled violently.

"Get out!" Sho'keh said, wanting these sun-dried assholes gone, one less problem to deal with. When he turned back, all their weapons were trained on Dallion.

"Fuck that, he's—holy shit—" The head rider yelled and let loose with his rifle. The others joined in, the desert night opening up with gunfire.

Sho'keh dove behind a large boulder, hoping the bandits wouldn't mess up Dallion's face too much for identification purposes. Dead or alive, he was getting that man to Albuquerque. He waited for the imminent pause of reloading, but with that pause, he heard some monstrous roar of rage. Then a high pitched human scream.

What he heard next sounded like a plate of spaghetti falling to the floor, a wet *splat*. A second later, Sho'keh nearly brained himself on the rock as something flew over the boulder and landed in front of him. It was the upper half of one rider, his innards trailing out from under him like confetti, fingers drumming up dust as they spasmed and groped the adobe beneath him.

More screams. A tearing sound like wet fabric. One more gunshot, followed by a feminine cry. A bestial snarl, the sound of something from the pit. Sho'keh steeled himself to peer from behind the boulder, knowing he was about to witness some unholy abomination. He cursed himself for not grabbing the rifle.

Sho'keh sighed, whispering to Fish-Ears, and came out from the boulder, his shooting irons leveled. His legs became rooted to the spot.

One rider remained standing of the original three. The one not ripped in half lay in a bloody, unidentifiable heap in the dirt. The other had popped a shot off at the misshapen thing that snapped its blood-flecked chops at him. Sho'keh saw the round punch into the subhuman's flesh, but it may as well have been a pebble flung at a grizzly bear. The Dallion-thing didn't even flinch, instead letting out another of those asshole-puckering snarls before leaping upon the rider, who'd turned to run. He got maybe three steps before it was on him. Sho'keh saw in adrenaline-dilated slow motion as the gore-caked, but sickeningly human-like face disappeared into the nape of the rider's neck.

Just as he saw a gleaming nub of spine ripped from the spasming rider, Sho'keh thought, damn the bounty. He opened up, the twin hand cannons firing off so quickly the multiple reports just bled into one another, a continuous thunderous roar until his guns clicked empty.

Sho'keh didn't wait for the gunsmoke to clear, he dove for the rifle, landing on his belly and clawing after it. He'd managed to hook one hand around the walnut stock when he felt the hand of god close around his foot, the hand of god apparently full of teeth and hot spittle.

The bounty hunter screamed as he was flipped over, feeling muscle and tendons rend in his foot, a hot thunderbolt of pain shooting up his leg.

He raised his head as he brought the rifle up, saw the twisted, naked form of Dallion peppered with leaking holes. *The bullets touch me, they just don't hurt.*

The figure loomed over him, stretched painfully enormous against every law Sho'keh knew. Crimson chops crinkled up in a snarl, huge yellow eyes peering down at him, as if considering whether to eat the bounty hunter all at once, or to savor him. Then something glinted in the dirt. The bounty hunter crabbed over to it backwards, as slow as a shadow.

"Treated you right, shared my kill with yuh. Go easy, now." Sho'keh said evenly, swallowing his terror as the unholy face quivered before him. Dallion took one step after another, soon almost hovering over his fleeing captor. The bounty hunter could smell the sour-meat stink of open flesh mending, and its breath, clouding through the fresh gore in the man's teeth. They stared at each other for a long moment, hunter and quarry reversed, regarding one another with unknown intentions.

Then, breaking the spell, the shape reared its head up, the jaws opening impossibly wide as Sho'keh felt the necklace between his fingers. Wicked teeth bloomed from open holes blasted away by gunfire, and he glimpsed the gobbets of skin and hair stuck in the gums, gleaming in the blood moon. He closed his scrabbling fist around the silver, and flung it into the gaping maw.

Dallion writhed like a horse-stomped viper, jaws cracking inward, his misshapen carcass receding into itself. Sho'keh snatched up the rifle and watched as the necklace shoved the man's flesh down the barrel of his ribcage, stuck again and again with God's own ramrod.

The bloody wreckage coughed raggedly, then made a final lunge for Sho'keh, disjointed anatomy wheeling. A bouquet of teeth bit down across cold rolled steel instead of his own noggin, and Sho'keh wrenched the rifle loose, tearing Dallion's face from the cheeks to the ear.

There was a muffled *whoomph* as the man's chest absorbed the blast. Dallion rocked back, a burnt keyhole where his heart should have been, then collapsed on top of his killer. What seemed like colossal weight to Sho'keh slowly ebbed away, and he bit his knuckle as not to scream. An amalgam of man and demon transmogrified and twisted with terrible, liquid sounds, until it was only Dallion's naked body draped over him. The bounty hunter shifted him, turning the rose blossom of his back to the ground.

Sho'keh sat back on his heels and stared around at the carnage around him, his mind spinning. The horses scattered. Pieces of dead men littered the desert floor around him, the fire still crackling. The spiders of Dallion's hands crawled up his sleeve to his collar, pulling hard.

"Shithead...you play a good...round," he said, looking up with black eyes. Pulling him closer with a last clutch of inhuman strength, Dallion whispered in his face with torn lips, then fell to pieces. The bounty hunter fished around in the cavity until he found the necklace, sticky with what once was the font of humanity.

Sho'keh sighed, flopping down at the rim of the fire. He took out the bottle of Ten High, hands trembling so badly he nearly dropped it. The whiskey sloshed against the glass, and the bounty hunter compared it to the shine of the silver, then strung it over his neck.

"San Agustin de la Isleta," he said, drinking deep, hearing voices in his head.

Nuttier than a pecan pie filled with squirrel turds, Frankin said.

Double ugly, toad feet, Fish-Ears said.

Death will forget you, Dallion said.

ABOUT THE AUTHOR

Richard Beauchamp resides just on the outskirts of the Missouri Ozarks, where he often spends most of his time hiking, fishing, camping, and doing his best to avoid people. He lives with his fiancé, their dog, and many cats. Richard's fiction has appeared in such esteemed publications as Dark Peninsula Press's "Negative Space" Survival Horror anthologies, Cohesion Press's "SNAFU" anthologies, and "Along Hallowed Trails" From Timber Ghost Press. His debut short fiction collection "Black Tongue & Other Anomalies" from D&T Publishing was a nominee for the 2022 Splatterpunk Awards for Best Fiction Collection.

For more information including a complete bibliography, media appearances, interviews and release schedule, visit Richard's website at www.richardbeauchampauthor.com

MORE FROM THIS AUTHOR

"Black Tongue & Other Anomalies" (From D&T Publishing)

"AUTONOMOUS" (Independently Published)

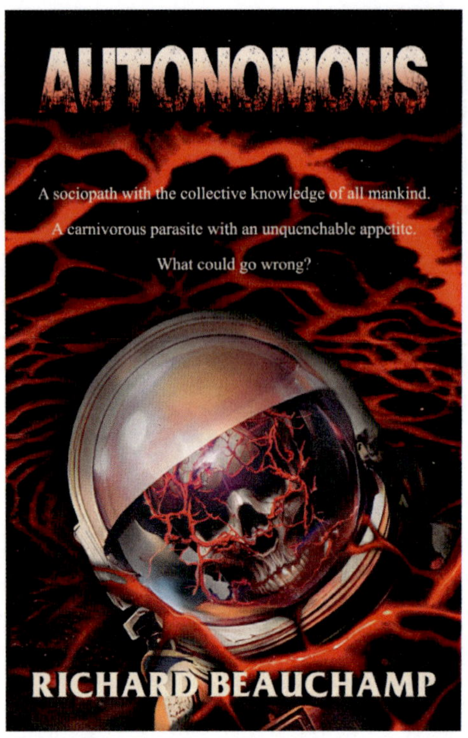

"SNAFU: Dead Or Alive" (Cohesion Press)

"Negative Space 2: A Return To Survival Horror" (Dark Peninsula Press)

Back
EDITED BY
ARIC SUNDQUIST
NEGATIVE SPACE 2
A RETURN TO SURVIVAL HORROR

Made in the USA
Monee, IL
24 March 2025

14552419R00043